THE GIRL FROM CLEVELAND CITY
EPISODE 3:
THE IDENTITY PARADE

Story and Screenplay by
ALEX SUKHOY

with Jacob Livshultz

©CREATIVE CADENCE LLC
GREATER CLEVELAND, OH
@CREATIVECADENCE

TELEPLAY
June 2024; 1st Edition 06/01/24
EARLY DRAFTS 2007 - 2024

This is a work of fiction. Except for the rage. That shit is real.

BRIDGE - EXTERIOR - DAY

TITLE CARD:

"Crime is terribly revealing. Try and vary your methods as you will, your tastes, your habits, your attitude of mind, and your soul is revealed by your actions."

- Agatha Christie

The Soundtrack of Duplicity

The title of Episode 3 - *The Identity Parade* - stems from the UK legal expression of the same name. The US English translation? The police line up.

If you've ever watched *any* crime/cop/detective show or movie then you've seen the scene: a group of five or six people, typically adult men, stand next to each other, each holding a number. They often look similar and are sometimes asked to say something, so that the victim, behind the glass with the detectives and legal team with them, could best identify who they think committed the crime.

Sometimes the victim makes the correct guess.

Sometimes they're so traumatized from the shocking event, their memory betrays them.

Sometimes they do point to the right perp and then that individual goes to trial. And then the defendant's lawyer - public or on retainer - does everything in their power to discredit the victim, or the witness, or both. It's their job to put the doubt into the minds of the jury. Unless the prosecutor meets the burden of proof the identified perp is found not guilty.

I know this well, from the thousands of hours of watching every episode of every season of every property in the *Law and Order* franchise, and also from two intense years of watching UK detective shows on BritBox.

I also know this legal process intimately from serving as a jurist on a hard-core multiple-charges criminal case here in Cleveland.

When the twelve of us couldn't agree on one charge, and were brought back to the judge, she repeated to us, "You must follow the law."

We debated that one charge for three days, before agreeing that while we believe that he "did it," the prosecutors did not in fact meet their burden. They did on most of the other charges, but not on that one.

We, the twelve of us, did our jobs: we watched, we listened, we discussed, we debated and we looked for truth. We paid attention to the facts. We pushed back on assumptions, opinions and conjectures. We held each other accountable.

This was nearly two decades ago, before meme-driven social media and highly-biased big media all but destroyed objectivity.

During these past twenty years our collective intellect has struggled, hard, to differentiate truth from fiction.

Not only is the media a mess, but also so many "artists" and "influencers" are using the music, art, writing and even choreography of the past (that's not yet in public domain) and, with small modification, releasing it as their own, often neither paying nor giving credit to the OA. Unless a lawsuit pursues, they get away with it.

And, while Artificial Intelligence first planted its roots in the books of Aldus Huxley and George Orwell, in 2022 ChatGPT and other programs began to collectively eat propriety content, often without consent, and spit out PhD level papers. And songs. And books. And art.

It's been quite a journey to determine who made what when.

What's original?

What's derivative?

What's AI?

What's real?

In *The Identity Parade* my goal was to make it hard to know who committed what crime.

And the soundtrack?

Well, I'll let you figure that one out.

EPISODE 3
THE IDENTITY PARADE
SOUNDTRACK

1. WATCHING THE DETECTIVES - DURAN DURAN
2. THE KILLING MOON - MATTHEW SWEET & SUZANNA HOFFS
3. SMOOTH CRIMINAL - ALIEN ANT FARM
4. FOLSOM PRISON BLUES - BRANDI CARLILE
5. LAWYERS, GUNS & MONEY - WALLFLOWERS W/JORDAN ZEVON
6. SUSPICIOUS MINDS - FINE YOUNG CANNIBALS
7. I FOUGHT THE LAW - THE CLASH
8. NOTHING COMPARES TO YOU - CHRIS CORNELL
9. ONE - MARY J. BLIJE
10. I FEEL YOU - JOHNNY MARR
11. LAZARUS - MICHAEL C. HALL
12. SO LONG, MARIANNE - JAMES
13. OUT OF THE BLUE - ROXY MUSIC
14. ROUTE 66 - DEPECHE MODE
15. IT'S ALL OVER NOW, BABY BLUE - MATTHEW SWEET & SUZANNA HOFFS
16. PERFECT DAY - DURAN DURAN
17. LOVE WILL TEAR US APART - DEPECHE MODE

#WHODUNIT

INSTRUCTIONS: PLAY WHILE READING.

FLASHBACK SCENE FROM EPISODE 1.
CREDIT LINE: Somewhere in Cleveland Morning June 9 2007.

EXT. DOWNTOWN STREET

Building on Euclid / East 9th is on fire. Cops, fire trucks, ambulance trucks keep arriving. Media trucks/ reporters near by. Chopper flying over. DETECTIVE DUSAN, now much older, wearing trench coat and hat, gets out of the car. Approaches FIREMARSHALL.

DUSAN
What do we have here?

FIREMARSHALL
Smell it.

DUSAN
Gasoline. Arson?

FIREMARSHALL
Definitely arson. No bodies inside.

DUSAN
(looking up, around)
Whatever secret was in that building, someone didn't want it to see the light of day.

Just as the FIREMARSHALL turned to go back in, CRASH! Glass panes start falling off of the building's original facade and come crashing on the sidewalk, splintering all over the place.

DUSAN bends down to pick one up, but sees something odd on the sidewalk. Picks it up. Looks at it. Shows it to FIREMARSHALL.

FIREMARSHALL
Human bone. Shit.

More human bone fall on the sidewalk. Dusan looks up the building, looks at the FIREMARSHALL. DUSAN's horrified because he knows exactly what is going on.

INT. POLICE STATION - DAY

DUSAN keeps staring at the board of characters: PATRICK, AARON, JACOB, SEAN, COLLEEN, MARY, JOSEPH. In the middle there's a circle with a big question mark. DUSAN's trying to make sense of all the connections. He's frustrated because he's missing the key detail that connects everyone.

DETECTIVE PORRELLO, female, late 30s, African American walks in.

DETECTIVE PORELLO
Any luck?

DUSAN
It was AARON and PATRICK who killed JOSEPH and then cemented him. But I'm not clear who set the building on fire.

PORELLO
Cui bono?

DUSAN
That's the thing. No one. No one benefits. The mafia days of Cleveland are long gone.

PORELLO
You know someone wanted that pyramid down.

DUSAN
But why? Why the risk? That building's been in Esti's family for decades. They weren't doing anything with it.

PORELLO
Maybe they got an offer they couldn't refuse?

DUSAN
Godfather fan?

PORELLO
Dad's Sicilian. Every Christmas after church while other kids opened presents, my family watched *The Godfather*.

DUSAN
Original or the sequel?

PORELLO
Both! One year we even had to watch the third one. But only that one year.

They both chuckle. PORRELLO looks at her watch.

PORELLO (CONT'D)
Speaking of which. Mom's dinner. She's going to kill me if I'm not there on time. You know how moms can get.

DUSAN nods. PORELLO exits. DUSAN's head starts spinning. The mom comment triggered him. He realizes that the one person he's overlooked in solving the crime. He pulls his wallet out. Opens it and pulls out a small photo. Slowly approaches the board. Picks up a thumbtack. And nails the photo to the center circle. Walks a few steps back. It's ESTI.

TITLE CARD: Somewhere in Cleveland. Late 70s.

INT. DR. OFFICE - DAY

ESTI is at the doctor's office. He's a middle aged Jewish man, wearing a keepa. Her legs are in stir-ups while a male doctor examines her, one hand on top of he stomach, the other inside her.

DOCTOR
Mazel Tov, Esti. Isaac is a big brother.

ESTI
(numb)
How far along am I?

The DOCTOR pulls his hands out of ESTI's body, takes off his gloves and washes his hands.

DOCTOR
(smiling)
Eight weeks.

ESTI, legs still up in stir ups, turns her head to her side and a tear comes down her cheek. She realizes the baby could be AARON's or could be JOSEPH's.

ESTI
What are my options?

DOCTOR
Gam zu l'tova. This, too, is for the good.

DOCTOR takes ESTI's legs off the stir ups and puts them back into the table. She is relieved from the discomfort and sits up a little. But then she realizes the true weight of the situation.

DOCTOR (CONT'D)
Esti. Listen to me. If there was anything wrong, then the Rabbis says we do what we need to save the life of the mother. But here, you, the baby, well, you're both in perfect health. If you do any harm to this child, it will be a sin against *Hashem*.

DOCTOR then turns around to wash his hands. While water runs ESTI sits frozen on that stark hospital table.

ESTI
(whispers)
And those who sinned against me? What about them?

DOCTOR
Did you say something, Esti?

ESTI slowly turns to him, then looks turns to audience, breaking the third wall.

ESTI
What I really want to tell him is about all my pain, all those who have sinned against me, about how my own husband couldn't protect me and how I would've never been in this situation if it wasn't for my narcissist mother and passive father.

Instead, I'm going to do what most women do in these situations. I'll drink another cup of regrets, guilt and shame and let it simmer in my soul, topping off the gallons of bullshit that others have served me.

ESTI, still looking directly into screen, pretending to lift a glass to toast.

ESTI (V.O., CONT) (CONT'D)
L'chaim, motherfuckers.

ESTI looks back at the doctor, attempt a fake smile.

ESTI (CONT'D)
Just thinking what to make for dinner tonight.

DOCTOR
That's natural. You're pregnant. Your mind, body, the hormones. Everything is changing. You're carrying new life inside of you. Growing your *meshpuha*. A true gift from *Hashem.*

ESTI, turns to audience.

ESTI V.O.
Except that I don't feel blessed. I feet cursed. Never once being able to live the life I want to live. My choices were made from the time I was born. No, conceived. From the moment I was conceived it was all decided.

Nothing determines more in your life than whose vagina you come out of.

DOCTOR
There's one more thing.

ESTI looks up at DOCTOR, in that deep level "now what" exhaustion that mothers deal with day in day out.

DOCTOR (CONT'D)
You and Aaron have truly been kissed by the angels.

ESTI
How?

DOCTOR
Ha-tov ve-ha-metiv. Twins. You're carrying twins, Esti! What a blessing.

ESTI hears this news, eyes slowly going from DOCTOR down to the ground. ESTI feels the shackles on her soul close in tight.

FLASHBACK SCENE FROM EPISODE 2

INT. DINING ROOM - NIGHT

Dining Room of JOSEPH's MOTHER's house. It's cleared except for a framed photo of JOSEPH resting on top of a vintage black lace table cloth.

JOSEPH'S MOTHER, an elderly dark skinned woman, is covered in black, head to toe, with a veil covering her face. She mourns her missing son. Her only son. Other family is there, some lighter, some darker. She's part Sicilian, part African American. JOSEPH has always passed for Sicilian.

We see the back of a MAN sitting directly across from JOSEPH'S MOTHER. Behind her hangs a vintage small painting of The Last Supper, a large cross and a black and white photo of JFK. There's also a framed map of Sicily. Next to the mystery man is a folded newspaper.

MYSTERY MAN
I know who did this to your son.

JOSEPH'S MOTHER sits, coldly. Motions everyone else to leave them alone.

MYSTERY MAN takes out folded newspaper and on the front page is a photo of AARON, smiling in front of his Euclid Avenue building development. The MAYOR is next to him.

Newspaper Headline: New Downtown Development Means Cleveland Jobs.

MYSTERY MAN (CONT'D)
It was AARON. At the construction site. Downtown.

JOSEPH's MOTHER looks down at the photo of her only son.

MYSTERY MAN (CONT'D)
I know of a way to balance the natural order of things.

JOSEPH'S MOTHER looks directly at him. Cold as ice. But curious.

MYSTERY MAN (CONT'D)
Aaron's wife. She's pregnant.

JOSEPH'S MOTHER is paying close attention. There's a sudden calculating look in her eyes. Just nods her head. MYSTERY MAN gets up. It's PATRICK. He's just double crossed ESTI, AARON and that entire family.

CREDIT LINE: SOMEWHERE IN CLEVELAND June 2007

EXT. STREET - NIGHT

DUSAN drives feverishly through the streets of downtown Cleveland. He presses the gas petal. He's stressed and starts perspiring.

INT. BEDROOM - NIGHT

COLLEEN holds SEAN Jr. while throwing laundry in. Checks pockets of everything. Notices how much SEAN's wardrobe has changed - lots of sport coat jackets, slacks, less jeans. She puts Jr. down and touches her husband's clothes, cascading her hands over the sleeves. She smells them and notices a scent. She then sees a bottle of expensive cologne on top of the closet shelf.

COLLEEN
(Whispers)
Who the fuck is she?

CREDIT LINE: SOMEWHERE IN CLEVELAND. FLASHBACK.

INT. HOSPITAL ROOM - DAY

Stark delivery room. Lots of bright lights. No photos or artwork. Just a cold room. Various medical equipment everywhere. ESTI's in a gown, on the hospital bed, her legs are in stir-ups. She's in labor. A MASKED DOCTOR enters the room, along with a MASKED STAFF.

ESTI
(confused)
Where's my doctor?

STAFF preps room for surgery, including needles with medicine, scalping knives, a rolling baby tray, bright lamps, towels, etc.

MASKED DOCTOR
He's...with another patient. A different delivery.

ESTI, about to deliver and knowing something is very, very wrong, looks stressed. She begins to perspire and the blood pressure machine begins to beep - it's escalating and quickly.

MASKED DOCTOR (CONT'D)
Don't worry, honey, I'll take care of you.

ANOTHER MASKED STAFF MEMBER briefly lifts her up and then injects an epidural into her spine, without even asking her. He then takes her arms and straps them down on the table.

ESTI
What are you doing? Where's my husband? STOP!!!!

MASKED DOCTOR
(in a fake comforting voice)
We need to do an emergency C-section. Everything will be ok.

MASKED DOCTOR then injects a needle into her arm and she slowly stops resisting, then closes her eyes. She's fully sedated.

EXT. STRIP MALL PARKING LOT - DAY. PRESENT

ESTI steps out of her black Mercedes and walks towards a restaurant door.

INT. MIDDLE EASTERN RESTAURANT - DAY

It's a local Arabic establishment. Dim lighting, hukas, mosaic table tops, Middle East rugs on the walls. It's 1:50PM, but the restaurant is rather full. As soon as she walks in, all the natives look at her and whisper things to each other. She clearly doesn't belong.

HOST comes up to her.

HOST
Can.. I help you?

ESTI
I'm meeting a friend here. At 2.

HOST takes two laminated menus and walks ESTI towards a tiny table towards the very back, by the kitchen doors. When plenty of other tables are empty. She does not make a fuss. She's spent her whole life living the outsider looking in.

WAITER brings ESTI a small bowl of humus and pita, and a Turkish coffee.

ESTI nods in gratitude. She picks up the tiny cup and sips the coffee. The best she's had in years. Looks around restaurant. The looks have stopped. The PATRONS are back to their own discussions.

Time passes. She looks at her phone. Nothing. She takes out a small leather notebook out of her Chanel purse. It's her diary. It's the only thing she's ever trusted.

Knowing she is in for the long wait, she begins to write a list:

Casino.

Casino.

Casino.

ESTI's mind begins to think back to a simpler time.

EXT. LAKEFRONT - DAY. (FLASHBACK)

Seventeen-year-old ESTI, a pretty white girl dressed in linen dress, pearl earrings and pearl necklace, and white headband in her dark hair, sits on lakefront bench overlooking downtown Cleveland.

Next to her sits eighteen year-old African American boy JOHN, who is dressed in second-hand but pressed pants and button-down shirt, and old, but polished shoes. He also has big brown eyes and a warm smile.

There's a clear economic difference between them. They like each other and found a quiet place away from their different worlds. There's an innocence between the two of them.

JOHN
I love you, Esti.

ESTI
I love you, too, John.

JOHN reaches for ESTI's hand.

JOHN (OPTIMISTICALLY)
Let's run away together. I'm serious. Let's go to New York. Everything's happening there. You can do your art...

INT. MIDDLE EASTERN RESTAURANT - DAY

ESTI snaps back into the present. Commotion is all around the restaurant.

Few minutes later, the entire staff lines up by the door to welcome their special guest.

The SHEIK walks in. His BODY GUARDS follow, but he motions for them to go back outside, which they do. The HOST welcomes the SHEIK and takes him to the very best table he has. ESTI watches all this. The SHEIK sees ESTI and walks right to her. ESTI gets up, they greet each other.

HOST
Sheik, if I had known she was your guest...

SHEIK sits down with ESTI at the small table in the back. Keeping his eyes on ESTI, and with one finger the SHEIK waves off the HOST, who now embarrassed, shrugs his body and walks to the front of the restaurant.

SHEIK
New generation.

ESTI
New generation.

SHEIK
How are your sons, Esther? I hear there's some marriage hesitation.

ESTI should be surprised but then she knows that nothing gets past this man. The SHEIK has eyes and ears everywhere.

ESTI
I don't want to pressure him.

SHEIK
The way your mother pressured you.

ESTI
Not just my mom. Both of my parents.

SHEIK leans in close to ESTI, looks her dead in the eyes.

SHEIK
Your father, may Allah rest his soul, he never wanted you to marry that man.

ESTI
John. He didn't want me to marry John.

SHEIK looks at ESTI in a both loving and scolding manner that a father may look at his own daughter.

SHEIK
Aaron. Abraham didn't want your marrying Aaron, your husband.

ESTI sits frozen. Of all the conversations to happen that day, this was on her list.

ESTI
What?

HOST walks up to their tiny table brings the SHEIK Turkish coffee and a large tray of appetizers. HOST directs WAITER to pull up another small table so that the large appetizer tray has a place to fit.

HOST
What else can we bring to you, Sheik, and to your guest?

SHEIK
Actually, I am her guest. And she is yours. Bring us your desserts.

The HOST and WAITER rush out.

SHEIK (CONT'D)
(to ESTI)
Don't tell my wife.

ESTI is still so shocked, she doesn't see anything happening in front of her. She is anxious.

ESTI
You were saying.

SHEIK
Ah, yes, Abraham. Aaron. You.

ESTI takes another sip of her coffee. She braces herself.

SHEIK (CONT'D)
Abraham. Your father. He didn't come from wealth. Your mother, she did. And she wanted what every woman from wealth wants.

ESTI
More wealth.

SHEIK
Of course.

ESTI
So, why did she marry my dad?

SHEIK
She was young. Her parents wanted her to marry Edgar.
(ESTI shrugs)
Edgar Miles Bronfman.

ESTI
The Seagram fortune?

SHEIK
Oh, yes, originally Canadian, how do you say that word...
(looks down, points to his shoe)

ESTI tries to understand what the Sheik is saying.

As SHEIK looks down at his shoes, he then sees ESTI's boots.

SHEIK (CONT'D)
Bootleggers! That's it!

SHEIK excitedly and almost laughing, explained the word so loudly, the rest of the restaurant patrons look in his direction. Then out of respect, smile and nod their heads.

SHEIK (CONT'D)
Bootleggers! I love that word. Tells you exactly a man's profession... so, yes, your grandparents wanted your mother to marry a rich bootlegger. But your mother, as you know, was not to be reckoned with. So she made a few calls to New York, where she had a friend, Ann. Ann Leiberman. And she made sure that Ann and Edgar met. They were as you Americans like to say of similar stock. Shortly after, Edgar and Ann got married.

ESTI looks more bewildered than ever.

SHEIK (CONT'D)
There was a time when your mother believed in love. And she loved your father. And she knew that he would always know that he was the lucky one. So she had all the power. He remained loyal to her till the end.

ESTI
So Aaron?

SHEIK
Aaron was supposed to grow your father's business. He was from New York. A lawyer.
(MORE)

SHEIK (CONT'D)
A real estate developer. This impressed your parents. At first.

ESTI sits there, like a grown child, learning where she came from for the first time.

SHEIK (CONT'D)
You know, my dear Esther, at your wedding, I had a few words with Aaron. And I asked him, "You came from New York to Cleveland. What exactly are you hiding from?" And you know what he said to me? He said, "I moved here for the opportunity." Stupid man. I told your father. I told your mother. They felt that shame and guilt for decades.

ESTI
So my marriage was a lie?

SHEIK
Show me an honest marriage...

SHEIK looks around restaurant, at all the people having a meal there.

SHEIK (CONT'D)
...and I'll show you a fool.

ESTI sat there. Betrayed and numb, all at once.

WAITER walks over, carrying two cups of tea in traditional cups. Puts each on the table. SHEIK turns to HOST. They both nod to one another.

SHEIK turns back to ESTI, then turns his right palm up towards the tea, looking at her.

SHEIK (CONT'D)
This calms my wife's heart.

ESTI picks up the cup of tea, sips it. Her shoulders relax.

ESTI
You're right.

SHEIK
Alkadhib lays lah 'arjul.

ESTI, mentally exhausted, looks at her watch.

SHEIK (CONT'D)
There's one more thing.

ESTI puts on her mental armor, prepared for anything.

ESTI
Do we have enough tea for this?

SHEIK
(smiling) Jacob.

ESTI
What about Jacob?

SHEIK
This girl he wants to marry. We looked into her family.

ESTI
Why?

SHEIK
Our of respect for your father, of course...

SHEIK lifts his hand and signals an exit.

SHEIK (CONT'D)
He will not marry her.

ESTI
(irritated)
Are you respecting my father or are you now being him?

SHEIK
They lost their shirts. The Moroccan casinos know how the mother likes her coffee. And...her men.

ESTI sits back on her chair. Watches all the restaurant customers coming in and out, eating their meals and heading back into their normal family lives. This normalcy she'll never know.

SHEIK (CONT'D)
I'm happy to ensure the daughter's exit out of Jacob's life.

ESTI
(nods)
I'll take care of it.

The SHEIK just looks at her. Patient. He knows. He's known her since she was born. Her father once saved his life. For this, the SHEIK's stayed loyal. And protective.

ESTI (CONT'D)
You know what? Yes. You take care of her.

ESTI sits back in her chair, like a warrior returning from war.

ESTI (CONT'D)
My chessboard is full.

SHEIK
Consider it done.

ESTI knows who she's dealing with. She sits back up.

ESTI
In return?

SHEIK smiles, sips his tea. He also knows who he's dealing with.

SHEIK
The Irish Bend.

ESTI exhales, nods and knows this is the outcome, whether she wants it or not.

SHEIK (CONT'D)
You will, of course, have your 10%. For life. Vlad will ensure it.

ESTI
Vlad? (pause) You're still in business with Putin?

SHEIK
A man must feed his family... He wants to close on the deal quickly.

ESTI
The oil?

SHEIK
What else is there? He wants to close quickly. So your money is all set.

ESTI
Why the rush?

SHEIK
(shruggs shoulders)
Vlad is a business man. He has an acquisition in mind.

ESTI
Crimea.

SHEIK
Crimea.

ESTI
1853.

SHEIK
And here we are.

ESTI
And here we are...and the Euclid property?

SHEIK
Your father came to me. In a dream...he doesn't want the secrets of that building unleashed into the world. I must respect his wish. You keep that.

ESTI
(surprised)
You're walking away from the casino?

SHEIK
Of course not. We will build it in the Irish Bend development.

ESTI nods.

SHEIK (CONT'D)
Your ten percent of casino revenue? That's my forgiveness fee on the Euclid Building.

ESTI understands and accepts this arrangement. She can convince and manipulate the decision makers of Cleveland. She can't go up against Putin.

The SHIEK gets up. The HOST opens the door outside. The SHEIK'S SECURITY GUARD walks in and heads towards the restaurant corner where the SHEIK stands.

ESTI also gets up, gathers her purse and sunglasses.

SHEIK (CONT'D)
If only more men had your wisdom and strength, my dear Esti. The madness between our people would end.

SHEIK raises his palms up and looks at the ceiling as though he's looking up at the sky.

SHEIK (CONT'D)
Sarah and Hagar.

ESTI
And here we are.

SHEIK
Shalom Aleihem.

ESTI
Salaam-Alaikum.

As the SHEIK and his SECURITY MAN exit the restaurant, ESTI heads into the WOMEN'S BATHROOM.

INT. WOMENS BATHROOM - DAY

Dimply lit small room, with Arabic details on the walls and flyers of restaurant events. There are 2 narrow stall doors.

ESTI walks towards the sink and looks at her face in the gilded-framed mirror.

She tries to absorb all of it. Takes a deep exhale, while holding her hands onto the sink.

Bathroom stall toilet flushes. She didn't realize someone else was in there with her. A YOUNG WOMAN comes out, possibly 17 years of age. Beautiful face, big brown eyes, long brown hair and dressed in black pants, long sleeves. Scarf around her head. She looks at ESTI.

YOUNG WOMAN
(shyly)
You're so classy.

ESTI
Oh, thank you, my dear.

The YOUNG WOMAN washes her hands.

ESTI (CONT'D)
Are you comfortable sharing your name?

YOUNG WOMAN
Azeena. It means...

ESTI
Beautiful. It means beautiful. I'm Esti.

The YOUNG WOMAN is both surprised and happy. She then tries to fix her headscarf. She's struggling a bit.

ESTI (CONT'D)
May I?

The YOUNG WOMAN nods. ESTI takes her scarf, wraps it perfectly. Both of them look at each other and themselves in the mirror.

YOUNG WOMAN
I hope one day I can be like you.

ESTI
(smiles)
Promise me something.

YOUNG WOMAN
Anything.

ESTI
No matter what happens, just be yourself.

YOUNG WOMAN
(looks down)
I don't know what that means. My parents tell me what to do and I do it. I don't know anything else.

ESTI
One day, you will find your strength. And when you do, use it. With all your might.

The two WOMEN both smile. Then ESTI opens the bathroom door and walks out. The YOUNG WOMAN looks around, looks under the stalls, makes sure no one else is there. She reaches into her shirt inside pocket and takes out a folded piece of paper. She unfolds it and looks at it. It's a photo of her and an young man, her age. He's wearing a *keepa* and a Star of David necklace. Their heads are close, but not touching, and they're both smiling, clearly happy and in love.

WOMAN'S VOICE
Zeena!

The YOUNG WOMAN suddenly hears her mother's voice. She quickly takes the photo, folds it back up and hides it inside her shirt's inner pocket. She also pretends to be fixing her headscarf.

ZEENA'S MOTHER walks into the bathroom. Looks around.

ZEENA'S MOTHER
Daena nadhhab!

ZEENA looks at herself in the mirror one last time. Whispers quietly to herself, "Be yourself."

INT. GYM - DAY

Crowded gym, full of athletic men and women. Everyone's in killer shape. Everyone's a C-Suite executive or a lawyer or both. JACOB's dressed in Adidas athletic wear, listening to music from his iPhone, runs on treadmill. Lean and full of muscle. TV screens all over the gym reporting various news channels. CNN, FOX, AL JAZEERA, MSNBC.

JACOB continues to run and sweat hard. As the WOMAN on the treadmill next to him gets off and wipes the machine, a YOUNG MAN his age hops on.

MIKE
Jacob.

JACOB
Mike.

MIKE
Looking good.

They both nod at each other in familiarity, and resume their workouts.

Suddenly, all TVs and smartphones report a news break. Some athletes ignore the news, others pay attention and listen to the screen.

CNN REPORTER
This just in. A major Cleveland company is making international news today. Rothstein Global has been charged with financial fraud, including money laundering, mail fraud and tax evasion.
(MORE)

CNN REPORTER (CONT'D)
The Rothstein family, known for their commercial real estate investments in Cleveland, New York, London and Casablanca, has been under investigation for years. According to our sources, an anonymous tip came in to the FBI, with evidence that led to the charge. More to this story after we return.

MIKE
Isn't that your fiancé's family?

JACOB stops his run. Watches the screen. Commercial break.

REPORTER
The Rothstein family, which goes back to Jewish mob boss Arnold Rothstein, has fled the country. It's our understanding that Scott, his wife Julie and their daughter Rebecca are all on their way to Morocco. Morocco has no extradition laws. We will keep you posted.

JACOB is beside himself. He feels free. Reaches for phone.

SCREEN SPLIT OF JACOB AND ESTI

JACOB
Mom. Did you see?

INT BEDROOM-DAY

ESTI, still in her suit, jacket off, holding/drinking a glass of wine with one hand, holding something else in another.

ESTI
I did.

INT GYM-DAY

JACOB
Did you do this?

INT BEDROOM-DAY

ESTI
No...yes.

INT GYM-DAY

JACOB
We're going to lose millions. The Casino? The Irish Bend? What are we going to do?

INT BEDROOM-DAY

ESTI opens her other hand. It's the butterfly hairpin that John gave her all those decades ago.

ESTI
You're going to go live your life. And be happy.

INT GYM-DAY

JACOB
What about the business? What about another Jewish heir? This was going to give us both.

INT BEDROOM-DAY

ESTI
Be free, my son.

INT GYM-DAY

JACOB gets off the phone, gets off the treadmill, doesn't see MIKE waving off to him.

INT BEDROOM NIGHT

ESTI looks at the butterfly in her hand. She then does the unthinkable. At least to her. She picks up the phone and sends a text: Come over.

INT GYM SHOWER DAY

JACOB stands naked under the shower, his head tilted back towards the shower head. With a gray sponge, he lathers his tall, strong body. Just as he's about to wash his genitals, just looks down at his cock. He washes it aggressively. It's now fully free. He's free. He slips down on the floor, in the shower corner and weeps.

INT DINING ROOM DAY

MAN'S HANDS eating corned beef boxty pick up and look at the phone.

MAN'S Hands text back: OMW!

EXTERIOR EUCLID AVENUE- NIGHT

Evening. Downtown Cleveland busy with traffic, pedestrians, tourists. VANs WARPED TOUR in town.

DARK BLUE BMW 3 SERIES heading west, and just crosses the intersection of Euclid and East 12th. Due to traffic, stops right in front of the Euclid Building that Esti's family owns. BMW is playing Garbage's "#1 Crush".

Heading East on Euclid Ave., a DARK BLUE JEEP WRANGLER approaches East 12th, and stops just short of the intersection, also right in front of ESTI's family building, but facing East. Car is playing, NIN, "Closer".

The drivers' windows are down.

The two songs blend perfectly in rhythm, and in message.

They look at each other. It's JACOB in the BMW, SEAN in the JEEP. They look at each other with contempt, but neither knowing why. They can't stop staring at one another.

The music envelopes them.

Cars behind them start honking. Each refocuses on the wheel and moves ahead.

INT. STUDIO APARTMENT - NIGHT

MARIANNE sits on the bed, smoking a cigarette. She's wearing a long loose t-shirt, with a black shiny bra strap teasing off of one shoulder. Dog collar still on. Keeps looking at her phone. She's frustrated, but also knows she must keep her cool. That is the nature of her relationship with this JACOB person. MARIANNE gets up, walks over to the small bar area in front of the kitchenette and pours herself a scotch.

Door knock.

JACOB
It's me.

MARIANNE quietly puts down the drink. Also puts out the cigarette.

JACOB (CONT'D)
I know I'm late. Please open the door.

MARIANNE heads towards the door. The hard-wood floor and her heels reveal to JACOB that she's standing right there. She says nothing.

JACOB (CONT'D)
Marianne, I'm sorry...It was work... And I got lost finding your place...I know, I know, you don't want to hear that.

MARIANNE looks thru the peep hole in the door and sees JACOB, looking handsome and disheveled all at the same time. Wearing his black Armani business suit and a black silk tie, he's starting to act desperate.

JACOB (CONT'D)
I'll do anything. Anything. Just please let me in. I have to see you.

MARIANNE hears all this. And takes her time. She knows how this game is played.

JACOB (CONT'D)
Beg, do you want me to beg? I'll beg. I'm getting on my knees.

MARIANNE waits a few more minutes. She needs JACOB to feel completely defeated. Emasculated. Inferior.

From the back, MARIANNE takes off her t-shirt and throws it across the room. Both shiny bra straps reveal themselves. She finally opens her door. JACOB is on the floor of an industrial building floor, in fetal position, on cracked black vinyl tiles, sandwiched between graffiti walls. He looks up at her. She's wearing a zippered leather corset, leather thigh-high boots. Long snake tattoo with its tongue out crawling up her right thigh. One hand behind her back. A silver cockring necklace dangling in front of her bustier.

JACOB (CONT'D)
May I enter?

MARIANNE remains silent. Looks at him. Steps outside her door and walks around him examining every inch. She then squats down, looks right at JACOB's face. He looks back at her with some level of hope, or hint, of acceptance. MARIANNE's face is right in front of JACOB's. She gently touches it. Her lips close to his.

Just as JACOB start to feel a sense of relief, MARIANNE snaps back into full height and with one hand points for him to get in, while with the other hand reveals a long whip. She whips the floor in a snap that echoes in the industrial space.

Jacob, still on his knees, crawls his way out of the hallway and into her dark studio.

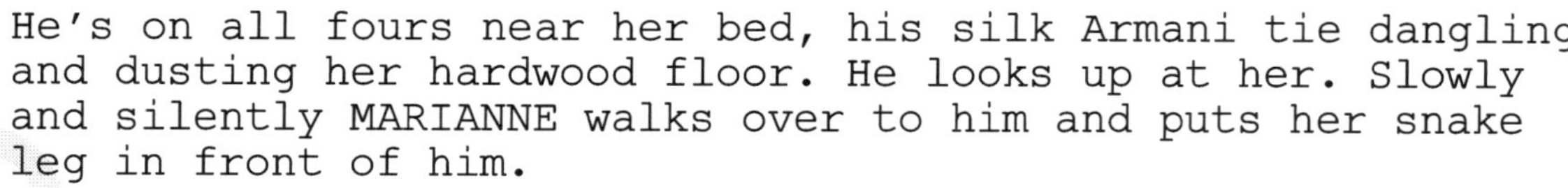

He's on all fours near her bed, his silk Armani tie dangling and dusting her hardwood floor. He looks up at her. Slowly and silently MARIANNE walks over to him and puts her snake leg in front of him.

JACOB looks up at her. And like a cat swirls around until his face is right in front of her boot. JACOB looks down and start to kiss the boot. He caresses and kisses that boot like it's a woman's breast. He then begins to lick it, his long tongue making love to this boot like his life depends on it.

MARIANNE snaps her whip again.

JACOB swirls around the boot and goes for the heel. He massages it, stroking every one of those 6 inches in full coverage. He then kisses it and licks it like a lollypop. JACOB then rolls over, his suited-up back on the floor, chest up. Looks up at MARIANNE, who looks down at him, signaling zero emotion. With the snake leg, MARIANNE steps on his white shirt. JACOB slowly opens his mouth. MARIANNE lifts her foot and slowly begins to penetrate JACOB'S mouth with her heel. JACOB licks it, holding her foot and starts to suck it off like a whore giving a proper blow job. Up. Down. In. Out. Short licks. Long licks. Repeat.

Whether or not MARIANNE is getting turned on, he'll never know. JACOB is however now in full erection. MARIANNE sees this. So she shoves the heel in even further, almost choking him. JACOB lets out a slight cough, but keep going.

Their eyes are glued on one another. Not one word exchanged.

MARIANNE glances over the giant bulge coming from the black Armani pants. Glances quickly back at JACOB and raises her right eyes brow. As if on cue, with her heel in his mouth, JACOB unzips his pants. No underwear. His cock full and free.

MARIANNE glances at him one more time. In three quick moves, she takes her heel out of his mouth. Squats down and sits right on top of him. Her corset designed for spontaneous fucking. She was now around him. He inside her.

JACOB wants to cum so badly.

MARIANNE tilts her head no. He doesn't yet have the permission to do so.

MARIANNE arches her back while her right hand grabs his black silk tie. She's riding him, hard. Tears open the buttons on his white cufflink shirt. His tan, muscled chest open. She then takes his tie off of him and ties it to the cockring. She puts the tie in his mouth.

As he pulls on the tie, attached to the cockring, attached to the leather bustier zipper, the slider begins to crawl down, revealing MARIANNE's skin.

MARIANNE arches her back further, reaching for the metal bar attached to the bottom of her bed. JACOB continues to fuck her and undress her, all at once. The zipper is fully undone and her breasts reveal themselves to him, nipples erect and now glistening from the sweat of the moment.

JACOB now pulls himself forward and puts his right hand around MARIANNE's naked waist, while with his left palm he slightly touches her right nipple. He feels the sensation rushing thru her body.

MARIANNE, still leaning back, both hands holding the bar, has fully surrendered herself to JACOB. The master has become the servant. JACOB's long hard tongue dancing on her breasts.

He then lifts his back off of the floor and while still inside her, tilts his body forward on top of hers, also grabs the bars and together they fuck in rhythm.

He looks her right in the eyes, and she looks back at him. MARIANNE opens her mouth, as she wants to say something to him.

He puts his finger on her mouth.

JACOB (CONT'D)

Shhhh.

JACOB can feel her pulsating. He nods his head, giving her permission to let go, to release, everything.

MARIANNE screams in an orgasm so loud her scotch glass shakes.

And, just as she surrenders in pleasure, he pulls her hands off the railing, and in one move, lifts her up, flips her over the bed and takes her from behind.

MARIANNE not knowing what's hit her, begins to reach a second orgasm. And seconds later they both hit peak. And collapse on the bed, onto each other, full of sweat and juice.

They both then fall asleep, in each other's arms.

And that night, JACOB and MARIANNE fell in love.

INT. BEDROOM - NIGHT

COLLEEN starts going through coat pockets. Doesn't find anything in the first or second coat. Third sport-coat she can feel something in the inside pocket. Takes out a business card. It's ESTI's.

EXT. ESTI'S PARENTS' HOUSE - NIGHT

SECURITY GUARD stands outside gates. Car pulls up and DUSAN gets out. Starts to head for the door.

INT. BEDROOM - NIGHT

Lavish large bedroom, with velvet curtains and matching velvet bedspread. SEAN and ESTI face each other. He touches her shoulder strap and it falls down. She looks SEAN in the eyes. They say nothing to each other. There's tension, sexual electricity and restraint. His machismo subsides and she takes over. They kiss and take off each other's clothes. He wants her but hesitates. He doesn't know what's come over him. He's never felt this kind of desire before. She notices this and lets him think he's in control. They're both naked, on top of the bed.

EXT. ESTI'S PARENTS' HOUSE - NIGHT

DUSAN approaches door, but two SECURITY GUARDS intercept him from entering. SECURITY GUARD stops him.

SECURITY GUARD
Password?

DUSAN pulls out his badge.

DUSAN
Fuck you. That's my password.

SECURITY GUARD reluctantly lets DUSAN in and reaches for phones to call ESTI.

INT. BEDROOM - NIGHT

ESTI is on top of SEAN, their eyes locked. He pulls her neck and head towards him and kisses her passionately. He takes the hairpin out of her hair and for the first time we see ESTI's long, dark hair cascade over her shoulders.

SEAN then works his way down on her body and slides towards the bottom of the bed.

SEAN hand holds down ESTI's ankle. His naked torso lying at the bottom of the bed. More moaning. SEAN kisses inside of ESTI's legs, first her left, then her right. SEAN inches up her thigh, his tongue exploring every inch of her responsive flesh. His hands then reach for her breast, massaging it, bringing her to arch her back up as he buries his face deep inside her thighs and stays there, delivering her extreme pleasure. Increasing moaning.

In sheer ecstasy ESTI howls a primal scream of orgasm reached, eyes still right into the camera.

ESTI exhales, turns to the nightstand and lights up a cigarette. Slowly exhales.

ESTI then looks right back at the camera, confident, relaxed and in on something.

As the camera pans up, SEAN lays on top of her, his head sideways on her belly, while her free hand covers his face as he lays still, in fetal position, like a content child.

SEAN
What is it about you?

ESTI says nothing. SEAN suddenly starts crying.

ESTI
What is it?

SEAN hesitates. He's embarrassed but he's also comfortable.

SEAN
It, it's you. You, you feel like home.

Door bursts open. It's DUSAN. ESTI looks. She's horrified. DUSAN is horrified. SEAN grabs his gun.

SEAN (CONT'D)
What the fuck?

DUSAN whips out his gun.

DUSAN
It's him, ESTI.

ESTI
What are you saying to me?

DUSAN
He's not dead. Your son is not dead.

PATRICK walks in.

SEAN
Uncle Patrick, what the fuck are you doing here?

UNCLE PATRICK
Seany boy, get your knickers on.

ESTI is in shock. JACOB walks in. MARRIANE follows.

Standing in the room are UNCLE PATRICK, JACOB, DUSAN and MARIANNE.

ESTI looks over to SEAN. She understands that it's her son and she also understands that she just made love to her own flesh and blood. She's just had a reunion with the most missing part of her life and she's also about to lose her mind.

SEAN can't move. He's paralyzed.

UNCLE PATRICK (CONT'D)
Put your gun down.

SEAN starts shaking, naked, on top of the bed and slowly as his hand quivers he puts down the gun.

There's screaming outside the door.

UNCLE PATRICK recognizes his daughter's voice and opens the door. COLLEEN runs in, holding SEAN Jr. Sees SEAN in bed with ESTI. Takes out her gun. Points it at ESTI while holding her son.

COLLEEN
Who the fuck is this bitch? I'm going fucking kill you. I'm going to kill both of you!

COLLEEN sees MARIANNE.

COLLEEN (CONT'D)
You fucking cunt. Still here. I should've fuckin' stabbed you.
(turns to SEAN)
What is this, Whore Day? You got all your whores in here today.

(MORE)

COLLEEN (CONT'D)
You and your goddam fucking mommy issues.

SEAN JR. reaches for UNCLE PATRICK.

SEAN JR.
Grandpa!

UNCLE PATRICK takes his grandson. DUSAN points his gun at COLLEEN.

DUSAN
Put your gun down. NOW!

COLLEEN
Not 'til I know who this old bitch is.

SEAN mumbles something.

COLLEEN (CONT'D)
What?

SEAN
(horrified)
She's my mother.

SEAN begins to weep. ESTI reaches for his gun and points it at her head.

DUSAN
(at Esti)
Don't do, ESTI. Don't do it!

PATRICK
Don't tell her anything, John.

JACOB just stands there trying to understand.

JACOB
What is going on here? Who is John? Mom, how do you know him?

DUSAN begins to slowly approach ESTI and tries to say the right things to her to get her to put the gun down. DUSAN finally reaches her and takes the gun out of her hand. He takes off his jacket and puts it around her shoulders.

ESTI leans into him and begins to weep.

FLASHBACK to DELIVERY:

TITLE CARD: Somewhere in Cleveland, mid 1980s.

INT. HOSPITAL HALLWAY - DAY

Nurse pushes wheelchair of woman in labor. Doctors are head-down in their clipboards. No one realizes what's going on.

AARON looks back anxious because his wife is in labor and he can't be there in the room with her.

INT. HOSPITAL ROOM - DAY

ESTI is unconscious and doctors are performing surgery on her. There's complications. Doctors in masks look at each other signaling what's next.

INT. HOSPITAL ROOM - DAY

ESTI still unconscious. Doctor holds up a screaming light haired NEWBORN.

MASKED DOCTOR
It's a boy.
(looks at the clock)
Born 10:27am.

INT. HOSPITAL ROOM - DAY

MASKED DOCTOR holds up a SECOND NEWBORN. He's dark haired and isn't screaming.

MASKED DOCTOR slaps him on his butt. SECOND NEWBORN lets out a scream. NURSE takes and holds the SECOND NEWBORN.

NURSE
Baby sex and time of birth?

MASKED DOCTOR
(sternly)
I'll take care of it. Go attend the next childbirth.

Only people left in the room are sedated ESTI, the MASKED DOCTOR and the TWO SCREAMING MALE NEWBORNS, facing each other.

Two minutes later, two MEN, dressed in black, faces not revealed, walk into the delivery room, with one carrying a large black bag. They open bag and inside is a blanket and a formula bottle. They take the light skinned boy and put him inside, then walk out.

INT. HOSPITAL WAITING ROOM - DAY

Silent scene.

Men of different ethnic backgrounds sit with their kids, waiting on the arrival news of all the new babies. AARON sits next to LITTLE ISAAC, waiting on the news. LITTLE ISAAC just stares at the clock in the waiting room. Since he saw his mother getting raped he's stopped speaking entirely. He's become a mute.

MASKED DOCTOR walks out. Tells AARON that he's the father of a healthy boy but that one boy is dead. AARON starts to hyperventilate. Collapses. MASKED DOCTOR quickly exits the scene.

NURSE runs towards AARON. Yells for doctor.

LITTLE ISAAC watches his father stop breathing.

Another DOCTOR runs up to AARON. Checks his pulse. Looks at clock. "He's dead. Time of death 10:35am."

LITTLE ISAAC kneels on the floor, lies down next to his dead father and hugs him, while looking back up at the clock.

EXT. OUTSIDE HOSPITAL - DAY

Two MAFIA MEN in dark suits walk out of hospital and get into limousine holding the FIRSTBORN BABY.

INT. HOSPITAL ROOM - DAY

ESTI, in the delivery room, holding her dark haired boy. Little ISAAC just sits there.

NURSES
She's not producing milk. The boy needs formula.

ESTI
(numb)
My son is dead. My husband is dead. I am dead.

INT. LIVING ROOM - DAY - EARLY 1980S

JOSEPH'S MOTHER's home. She sits in black, still in mourning over her son. The same male figure from before tells her

PATRICK
It is done.

PATRICK is the double agent who orchestrated the kidnapping of ESTI's first son, while they thought he died.

PATRICK (CONT'D)
There's something else.

JOSEPH'S MOTHER looks at him. Says nothing.

PATRICK (CONT'D)
It's Aaron. He's had a heart attack. He's gone.

JOSEPH'S MOTHER
(genuinely sad)
Sfortunato.

INT. FOSTER HOME - DAY (FLASHBACK)

A Catholic foster home. It's dreary. Lots of nuns. A baby boy wearing a blue shirt with a sailboat on it and baby girl wearing a yellow shirt with a bird on it are both placed next to each other, as new deliveries.

TITLE CARD: 6 MONTHS LATER

INT. FOSTER HOME - DAY (FLASHBACK)

The baby boy, a few months older, wearing the same shirt, with it being very tight/small on him, gets picked up and taken away. The baby girl in the exact same shirt, also small on her, is left alone.

INT. MENTAL HEALTH FACILITY - DAY (FLASHBACK)

LITTLE ISAAC sits on top of his bed and looks out the window. Doesn't say a word. ESTI and PATRICK are both in the room. BABY JACOB is in the stroller. Starts crying. ESTI gives ISAAC a quick hug.

ESTI
Say goodbye to your brother, JACOB.

ISAAC just looks at the baby, says nothing and keeps looking out the window, in silence.

INT. ESTI LIVING ROOM - DAY (FLASHBACK)

Private Bris for ESTI's newborn son, JACOB. RABBI is there, along with PATRICK. So is LITTLE ISAAC. No one else. RABBI begins procedure, ESTI looks away. She can't watch it. Sees photo of her and AARON, on their wedding day. AARON smiling happily, while she faked her best camera bridal pose. RABBI motions prayer over baby. ESTI is now a widower with two sons, and a business. She trusts no one. She has no one.

INT. BEDROOM - NIGHT

JACOB and SEAN face each other, brother to brother, for the first time. They then look at MARIANNE, the woman they've both been sleeping with. They realize she could be their half sister, on their father's side. MARIANNE and COLLEEN realize that they are half sisters, on their mother's side. ESTI realizes that all this time PATRICK has known everything.

ESTI
You, you did all this?

PATRICK
Esti, sweetheart...

ESTI
(anger growing)
You knew. All this time.

PATRICK
(slowly approaching ESTI)
I was trying to protect you.

ESTI
By kidnapping my son?

ESTI looks at SEAN in bed with her. She's horrified. Shocked.

ESTI (CONT'D)
I just slept with my own son.

SEAN starts crying.

ESTI's rage escalates to Mach 1 level.

ESTI (CONT'D)
You monster. You fucking monster.

ESTI lunges out of bed, right at PATRICK, wearing only DUSAN's jacket. She points her gun at PATRICK.

PATRICK
If I didn't kidnap your firstborn, you would have lost both of your kids. Joseph's mom assumed Aaron killed him.

ESTI
Aaron? Aaron didn't know how to protect me. IIIIII killed JOSEPH. I did it. And I should've killed you, too.

EVERYONE turns to ESTI, stunned.

PATRICK
You threw him out the window?

ESTI
(gun still pointing at Patrick)

ESTI (CONT'D)
Of course I did. He raped me. And none of you bastards were going to do anything about it.

ESTI (CONT'D)
You thought Aaron killed him? Aaron with his weak heart and his spineless excuse for a man. Please. Aaron had no fucking balls.

ESTI (CONT'D)
Where was Aaron when Joseph raped me? Where was Aaron when his son stood and watched?

DUSAN
(devastated)
You set that fire.

FLASHBACK CLEVELAND EARLY 1980s.

INT OFFICE BUILDING - NIGHT

JOSEPH survives the elevator ride. Says his prayers. Walks towards open window. Tears apart the list. ESTI, in her trench coat, lurks on in the corner. She knows that building inside out. She sees JOSEPH standing there, while holding her gun. Rethinks her methods. Puts the gun back in her coat pocket. Takes a running start and with all her might runs towards JOSEPH and pushes him out the window.

In her adrenaline rush, ESTI avoids looking out the window and instead beelines towards a secret back elevator, with a regular office door in front of it. It requires a special key. Her hands are shaking as she keeps trying to put it in the keyhole. She knows the men will show up momentarily. She finally takes a deep breath, slowly inserts the key and the old elevator door opens, ESTI walks in and pushes the first floor button. The elevator doors keep opening and closing. She's hearing the other elevator "ding", grasps her gun, and just as she hears footsteps, her elevator doors finally shut. Once the elevator stops on the first floor, and the elevator door creaks open, she runs thru the alley in the back of the building. She sees the flashlight reflect in the shiny garbage containers. Turns around briefly, then turns back, runs across Chester Avenue and gets into her car.

As ESTI drives home, she opens the window and lets out a primal scream that in her head echoes across all of Cleveland, Ohio, the Midwest, America and the World. It's the primal scream every mother births the moment she understands everything that is not at stake and that motherhood is the sword women die on. No matter what decisions or choices they make.

INT. BEDROOM - NIGHT - PRESENT

EVERYONE in the room watches ESTI, naked, in bed, her always perfectly coifed hair undone and unruly, cascading on her shoulders, with a gun, and they can't believe what they are hearing. Who is this woman? Who is she really?

ESTI
After everything I've been through and after all those fucking monsters did to me?

What else was the world going to take away from me?

PATRICK
(slowly)
Calm down, Esti. It's ok.

ESTI
Fuck you, Patrick. I'm not done. You, YOU and your swinging dick. And Joseph's swinging dick. All of your swinging dicks. Fucking anything that moves.

ESTI gets up and walks over to PATRICK. Takes his hand and puts in on top of her genitals.

ESTI (CONT'D)
Is this what you want? Pussy? You want my pussy? Lord knows you've had everyone else's in this town.

SEAN doesn't flinch from the bed. He's in a state of shock. COLLEEN is the only one in the room who, while holding her son, understands everything ESTI is saying, and still hates her.

ESTI (CONT'D)

Take it. Aaron did. My parents gave my young pussy to him. Joseph did. He just took it. In front of my son. So your turn, you Brutus. You already took my child. So take it. Take it!

ESTI, keeping PATRICK'S hand on her genitals point her gun to PATRICK'S head. PATRICK looks genuinely scared.

EXT. CONSTRUCTION SITE - DAY. FLASHBACK.

Cement truck, CONSTRUCTION WORKERS. Cement used to attached black glass panes to gorgeous century old building facade. PATRICK supervises. CONSTRUCTION WORKERS putting up panes notice the bones and body parts. They look at PATRICK. PATRICK just looks at them, nods to keep going. So they attach the glass panes to the facade with the bones and body parts sandwiched in between.

INT. BEDROOM - NIGHT

Back to the present where ESTI, SEAN, COLLEEN, MARIANNE, DUSAN, SEAN JR., JACOB and PATRICK all stand there not sure how to process anything that's going on.

ESTI still points gun at PATRICK. COLLEEN points gun at MARIANNE. SEAN weeps. DUSAN holds gun, not sure where to point. SEAN JR starts crying and runs loose.

PATRICK
ESTI, this is your grandson.

ESTI looks at SEAN JR. Still holds gun. Starts crying.

BLACK SCREEN. GUN SHOT.

HOLLYWOOD ENDING

TITLE CARD: CLEVELAND. TWO WEEKS LATER.

INT. DIVEBAR - NIGHT

DUSAN walks in. Sits at bar. BARTENDER surprised to see him.

BARTENDER
John. We haven't seen you since Bush was president. Sr.

DUSAN
(nods)

DUSAN pulls out his wallet. Takes out a small worn out square paper, which has the AA coin taped to it. Runs his fingers over it. Flips it over. 30-something year old photo of him and ESTI, young, happy and in love. DUSAN stares at it. Looks around the bar. Watches a thuggish 30-something guy follow a a 20-something giggling blond girl to the bathroom and slam the door.

BARTENDER
What's your poison, John?

DUSAN sits there, thinks about it.

DUSAN
Vodka. Straight up.

BARTENDER
You sure?

DUSAN nods.

BARTENDER pours him a shot.

DUSAN contemplates it. Looks at the photo. Picks up the glass. Brings it up to his lips. Then puts it down. Takes the photo with the taped AA coin, throws it into the glass, gets off the barstool and walks away.

TITLE CARD: CLEVELAND. SIX MONTHS LATER. MUSIC MONTAGE.

INT. AIRPLANE - DAY

COLLEEN and SEAN JR. board a plane and take their seats. There's and empty seat next to them. Plane fills up. SEAN JR. falls asleep in COLLEEN's arms. COLLEEN looks up and sees familiar face.

MARIANNE puts her bag on top and then sits down next her. She puts her hand on her stomach.

COLLEEN looks down at MARIANNE's big belly and then into her sister's eyes and realizes that she's pregnant. Either JACOB or SEAN could be the father.

The two SISTERS smile, say nothing and look ahead to their new life.

FLIGHT ATTENDANT
Ladies and gentlemen, please fasten your seatbelts. We'll be taking off shortly here. Our ETA is 6AM Dublin time. And enjoy your flight to Ireland.

Just behind the two women are both JACOB and SEAN, uncomfortably trying to act brotherly. Knowing everyone here sitting on this plane is family, related one way or the other.

SEAN JR peaks out of the seat and waves. Hi, UNCLE JACOB. JACOB looks at his nephew, looks at SEAN. There's finally a smile.

Plane takes off.

EXT. CLEVELAND IRISH BEND - DAY

CROWD of people at the Irish Bend. MAYOR SCALISH is there, the PRESS, the SHIEK. They are there to break ground on the new development. Applause. ESTI stands next to the SHIEK.

SHEIK comes up to the microphone. Begins...

SHEIK
Thank you to the hard-working people of Cleveland, and of course, your country, America.

Audience applause.

I first want to show my gratitude to my good friend ESTI, without whom none of this would be possible.

He turns and points to her. ESTI, Chanel suit and sunglasses on, modestly smiles and nods her head.

SHEIK (CONT'D)
Today is a new day. And the Irish Bend, built on the backs of immigrants, who wanted a better life, it's going to thrive again.

Audience, politicians applaud.

INT. HOSPITAL - DAY

PATRICK is in a wheelchair and doing some exercises. He's recovering from getting shot in the leg. He wheels himself to the window and sees Downtown Cleveland skyline. Contemplates his life and the mistakes he's made.

INT BAR - DAY

ISAAC is dressed in jeans and a polo shirt, sitting at the same bar and booth that JACOB and REBEKAH were once planning their wedding. Enjoying his very first beer in decades. Looks over at FEMALE BARTENDER. FEMALE BARTENDER looks right back at him. They hold eye contact for a few seconds.

YOUNG WOMAN, late 20s, sits down at the bench seat across from him. They both smile at each other.

YOUNG WOMAN
So you were telling me about your favorite movie..

ISAAC
Yes, have you ever heard of The Third Man?

YOUNG WOMAN
No. Tell me about it...

The two of them continue in conversation.

INT. HOSPITAL - DAY

NURSE
How are we doing today?

PATRICK
We? We are alive!

Smiles.

EXT. WATERFRONT - DAY.

Waterfront with dwarfed city scape with. Sixty-something ESTI, dressed in black pants and black sweater, with white coat and sunglasses, hair pulled back sits on park bench overlooking the water.

Next to her sits sixty-something JOHN, who is dressed in black slacks, a black Polo sweater, tan coat, also sunglasses. No hat.

There's very little difference between them. They like each other and found a quite place away from their once different worlds. There's no innocence left between the two of them. Just truth.

Young INTERRACIAL FAMILY walks by. KIDS make funny faces to the older couple on the bench.

ESTI waves back and smiles. JOHN makes funny face right back at the KIDS, who then laugh.

BUTTERFLY lands on ESTI's hand. JOHN and ESTI both look at the butterfly, smile. ESTI puts her head on JOHN's shoulder. They are finally together. They are finally happy. They get up off the bench and walk along the water, arms around each other.

As the BUTTERFLY takes off into the sky the camera follows it. The city scape becomes more clear. It's New York City.

FADE OUT. CREDIT

N O I R   E N D I N G

TITLE CARD: CLEVELAND. TWO WEEKS LATER.

INT. DIVEBAR - NIGHT

DUSAN walks in. Sits at bar. BARTENDER surprised to see him.

BARTENDER
John. We haven't seen you since Bush was president. Sr.

DUSAN
(nods)

DUSAN pulls out his wallet. Takes out a small worn out square paper, which has the AA coin taped to it. Runs his fingers over it. Flips it over. 30-something year old photo of him and ESTI, young, happy and in love. DUSAN stares at it. Looks around the bar. Watches a thuggish 30-something guy follow a a 20-something giggling blond girl to the bathroom and slam the door.

BARTENDER
What's your poison, John?

DUSAN sits there, thinks about it.

DUSAN
Vodka. Straight up.

BARTENDER
You sure?

DUSAN nods.

BARTENDER pours him a shot.

DUSAN contemplates it. Looks at the photo. Picks up the glass. Brings it up to his lips. Crumbles the photo and drinks his vodka.

TITLE CARD: CLEVELAND. SIX MONTHS LATER. MUSIC MONTAGE.

INT. AIRPLANE - DAY

COLLEEN and SEAN JR. board a plane and take their seats. There's and empty seat next to them. Plane fills up. SEAN JR. falls asleep in COLLEEN's arms. COLLEEN looks out the window and looks at Cleveland for the very last time. She's done.

FLIGHT ATTENDANT
Ladies and gentlemen, please fasten your seatbelts. We'll be taking off shortly here. Our ETA is 6AM Dublin time. And enjoy your flight to Ireland.

INT BAR - DAY

MARIANNE tending bar, helping her customers. She stretches her back as it hurts.

Behind the bar we see she's pregnant.

EXT. CLEVELAND IRISH BEND - DAY

CROWD of people at the Irish Bend. MAYOR SCALISH is there, the PRESS, the SHIEK. They are there to break ground on the new development. Applause. There's no sign of ESTI and another investor is there.

EXT. CEMETARY - DAY

PRIEST and the GROUNDSKEEPER stand in front of a coffin. No one else is there. PRIEST opens bible and reads.

PRIEST
"Patrick Francis Quinn. Eternal rest grant unto them, O Lord, and let perpetual light shine upon them. May their souls and the souls of all the faithful departed, through the mercy of God, rest in peace. Amen.

COFFIN lowers.

INT. MENTAL FACILITY ROOM - DAY

ISAAC looks out the window. Camera moves to the room next door. There is SEAN, also dressed in khakis and a white t-shirt, also staring out the window. He had sex with his mother, who, right as he was born, killed his father. The two brothers finally have the opportunity to get to know each other. In the mental facility. JACOB and ESTI, now dressed in black slacks and a black turtleneck, stand in the room with them. The whole family, fucked up and together.

JACOB looks at his mother, still doesn't comprehend anything.

JACOB looks up at ESTI. ESTI looks at all her boys. Kisses both ISAAC, SEAN and JACOB on their foreheads. Takes something out of her purse and holds on to it.

ESTI
I love you, my sons. All of you.

JACOB sits down next to his brothers and the three all look out the window and see the Cleveland City scape in the distance, with Lake Erie in between.

ESTI walks out alone. Walks thru hallway of mentally ill people.

ESTI (CONT'D)
(breaking 4th wall, talks directly to audience)
Jacob never really understood my life or my choices. How could he? He doesn't know my story.

Begins to perspire. Loses her balance. NURSE runs up. ESTI straightens herself out and continues to walk and talk to camera.

ESTI (CONT'D)
Most children don't want to know anything about their parents before they became parents. That part of their life is irrelevant to the offspring.

ESTI puts her right hand on her chest, over her heart.

ESTI (CONT'D)
(panting)
But, then...who really knows anything about mothers?

Half-way down the hallway, she loses her balance and collapses. NURSES and AIDS run to her and check her pulse. Look at watch. We can see them looking at clock, declaring her dead, but can't hear them as music drowns it all out.

SEAN, JACOB and ISAAC look out of their rooms to see the commotion and run towards their mother. Everything slows down. ISAAC looks at his dead mother. Looks back at clock.

ESTI's hand opens up. It's the butterfly barrette.

FADE OUT. CREDIT

Crawling Out Of The Sewer

First Published: March 25, 2018

Each time I watch *The Third Man* I discover something new. This past weekend, while catching the third act of this classic Noir, I came across two new observations:

1. Scorsese paid homage to a key post-funeral scene by replicating the same scene in *The Departed*

2. The physical and visual intensity of our protagonist running around and then trying to get out of the post-war Vienna sewer while he's being chased by military police is a beautiful metaphor for many of our favorite Noir characters: even if they are not in the sewer itself, their moral compass certainly is.

Orson Welles, as Harry Lime, who waters down medicine that then kills the very children whose mothers survived the bombs, is both monster and charmer.

Charming monsters are the scariest.

Because they live their lives keeping one foot in the sewer while the other (to paraphrase Ruth Bader Ginsburg) on our necks.

I thought about that, and the theme of water in *Chinatown*, the lost, haunted boat in *Deep Calm*, the tormented relationships in *Mystic River*. What is it about water - whether it's above ground or under ground, nature-made or man-made, that can go from safe to threatening within a split second?

One of the plot lines of *The Girl From Cleveland City* screenplay involves a lakefront development. Positioned to be the exciting, new place to live, work and play in the 216, that original story goes all the way back to when I first arrived here in 2003 and met the then Mayor Jane Campbell. Back then she was talking about doing something here "like in Chicago." After her talk I came up to her, shook her hand, introduced myself as a freshly minted MBA who grew up in Chicago, gave her my card and offered my help. I never did hear from her, but it does look like 15 years later that development is finally happening.

In a life-imitates-art-imitates-life cycle, the waterfront development in Cleveland City takes place in the present. And as with any development on an important piece of land, there must be first be a government-approved clearing. Then? There must be digging. And when you dig what will you find? The secrets of a city.

There's an Argentinian proverb a friend from business school once taught me: If you go looking for shit, you will find shit.

Well, I challenge that proverb to say that sometimes it's time for the shit to surface. Because its stench can no longer hide. Not under any number of layers of land or gallons of water.

Because sometimes even the most self-righteous, self-important and self-sacrificial characters are actually no better than the rats running around in the sewer, gnawing other people's lives and doing so with charm while wearing expensive coats and being loved by the women who took pity on them.

This is the essence of Noir. This is the essence of *The Girl From Cleveland City.*

Film Noir Love: Someone Always Gets Derailed

Originally Published: November 12, 2017

"Young mothers love me even ghosts of

Girlfriends call from Cleveland

They will meet me anytime and anywhere"

- "Day I Die" by The National

In any great film noir, there's a love story.

Double Indemnity.

Mildred Pierce.

Blade Runner.

The commonality they all share is that is in each tale of passion, heat and killer dialog, one party loves the other more. In some cases, they're not loved back in return. At all. Worse off? The man or woman to whom they give their hearts and give up everything have simply used them as a means to an end. Once the desired outcome is achieved those fallen into the swoon of it all are left with nothing. Sometimes sent to jail. And in the most tragic noir? They die.

There is no riding into the sunset together.

When it comes to showing the pain of heartbreak, visually and viscerally film noir works stronger than any other genre.

Recent studies have shown that in bad break ups, the heart has the same physical reaction as though it was physically damaged. Similar to a heart attack.

When on the other end of the relationship stick, you feel run over. You feel derailed.

And that then changes everything. It shifts the direction and dynamics of your life. Some get over it. Some get gone with it. And some are just gone.

In *The Girl From Cleveland City*, we meet Detective Dusan. Back in the 1970s he was a rising star on the Cleveland Police Force. A by-the-book officer who crawled his way out of a public housing and a crime-infested neighborhood, he then committed his life to putting bad guys behind bars and to cleaning up his community.

He was on path. He was on duty. He was on track.

But then he was blinded by the light of love. She was his everything. By the time she was done with him? He was left with nothing.

He spent the next twenty years a barfly at The Theatrical on Short Vincent Street, keeping on pulse with the city's back alley and boardroom dealings. But he never regained his momentum. He never got married. He remained loyal to the bottle.

And on that fateful June 2007 night, in Cleveland, that night he got called in to examine a fire in an old Downtown building?

That fire reignited his career. And brought him right back to his *Sliding Doors* moment.

Will his great love make the bus this time?

Every Day is Halloween: In Noir, All Characters Wear a Mask

Originally Published: October 29, 2017

"You think you can catch Keyser Soze? You think a guy like that comes this close to getting caught, and sticks his head out?" - Kevin Spacey, *The Usual Suspects*

It's Halloween weekend. Across the country, kids and adults alike are dressing up in costume, trick or treating and attending parties galore. Wearing a costume and, especially a mask, is holiday tradition, one that passes generation to generation. Superheroes, monsters, sexy nurses and the latest political and pop culture references serve as muse for All Hallow's Eve.

For the characters in Film Noir, to quote the band Ministry, "everyday IS Halloween." We, the audience, rarely know who is the hero, who is the monster and who is both. Sometimes we guess and feel good about ourselves and our deductive intelligence. And sometimes we're so surprised, no shocked, that we shiver in flashback, thinking how could we have possibly missed that detail. Remember Verbal Kint?

This is one of the biggest reasons why I love Noir. Because it's the most honest of all genres. It's not just about realism. It's about reality. And the struggle of the human condition. Any ideal citizen, when squeezed, pressed and desperate can be motivated to commit a crime. Prohibition fostered criminal activity. It made criminals ok neighbors because if having an alcoholic drink tipped the scale from good to bad then how can anyone ever really live up to the Great American Standard?

We all wear our masks. Because we all have secrets. We've all lied. Sometimes to others. Sometimes to ourselves. Self-denial is the very worst kind of deceit.

As I was working on my Cleveland script tonight, at Nighthawk, named after the famous noir-ish painting, while researching the genre - there's always so much more to study and learn about Film Noir - I suddenly realized that I had a new homework assignment to complete. I had to think about what secrets my characters are keeping.

And so in one of my two themed notebooks (one is for notes on the genre and Noir films I watch, the other is story notes for the screenplay, including characters, theme, setting, structure and making sure all the details in Act 1 drive a surprise twist pay-off ending in Act 3) I picked up my Sharpie and started listing all the key characters and then in the next column what one big secret each is keeping. Of course there's things they don't even yet know about themselves. That's the job of a good story.

The arc of the characters. But first and foremost, in Noir, we have to be very clear on what everyone is hiding. What mask they are wearing?

At least the writer needs to know this. And I'm so happy that as of tonight I know what each of their secrets is. And how all these characters have woven a web of deceit and duplicitous behavior that is no longer sustainable. It's about to implode.

Their masks are finally coming off.

THE GIRL FROM CLEVELAND CITY EPISODE 3

ESTI'S FAMILY TREE

Who the fuck even knows?

The Pitch (updated since Episode 2)

End Goal: A woman-directed and produced multi-episodic series distributed by a major streaming channel.

Genre: Neo-Noir

Theme: The rage of a mother.

Inspirational Films: *Chinatown* meets *Jade*

Setting: Cleveland 2007

Logline: A society page matriarch fights to protect a secret that can tear apart her family and take Cleveland down with it.

Tagline: Love, Crime and other Midwest Values

Story Relevance: We are Living in Noir Times

· From 2008 - Now, an economy that never re-stabilized while also launching the really rich into space.

· From Hollywood to Washington DC, tales of sexual, physical, emotional and professional abuse, ending our blind trust in the patriarchy. Epstein's Little Black Book unrevealed.

· From Alexa and Siri having key access into our homes, to devices recording (and recoding) our every behavior, to smart homes, and now the Meta Universes and content creator ChatGPT, technology has penetrated our work, wallets and wander.

· From retailers offering up fresh new inventory of disposable furniture and fast fashion to endless dating apps offering fresh and disposable men and women, ready, willing and able to do whatever is asked of them. And then, do it, again, again and again.

· From minimum wage stagnation to the erosion of full-time jobs, we're now glorifying the highly unstable and unreliable gig economy.

· From Cleveland once standing as the 5th largest city in the nation to 2020 Cleveland named as the Poorest City in America.

· In 2021 from fighting climate change to fighting the Great Plague to fighting racism to the exponential acts of public anti-Semitism, Twitter (X) reminds us daily of how much we fight.

· January 6, 2021: The Insurrection on our Capitol.

· February 24, 2022: Putin invades Ukraine, my birth country, during my birth month. The following month he invades my birth city of Kyiv.

· November 20, 2022 - ChatGPT Initial release Date

· June 24, 2022: Across states, Roe vs. Wade overturned. Rape victims, incest survivors, 15 years-old girls, ectopic pregnancy carriers and otherwise physically, mentally and fiscally endangered women forced into labor.

· January 2023: Book Banning in schools.

· February 2023: Spy Balloons.

· October 7, 2023: Hamas murders 1800 Jewish souls at a music festival. Takes hostages, including babies. Rapes, tortures, murders and parades women around town. Attacks Holocaust survivors.

· October 8, 2023: Anti-Semitic rhetoric and violence unleashes across US college campuses and across the world.

· November 29, 2023: "Irish Lives Matter" graffiti in Belfast Northern Ireland is declared a Hate Crime.

· December 1, 2023: "The House...voted to expel embattled Republican Rep. George Santos(cbsnews.com) Report points to fraud.

· **2024: What is Reality?**

Thank you for taking the time to read this.

Next:

A book of essays called *Alex After Dark*.

Thank you, Melyssa, for the title.

ACKNOWLEDGMENTS

Thank you, Cleveland City.

You gave me a home.

You made me return.

Twice.

You made me a Mother, Author, Entrepreneur, College Professor and Artist.

To every single film industry person who, over the years, has read any version or portion of this, and gave me constructive notes that, at those times, could have easily made me stop and quit, thank you for respecting these characters enough to ensure they lived the right story:

Barri Evins, Amy Salko Robertson, Phil Eisner, Evan Lieberman, Jimi Izrael, Tyler Davidson, Peter Lawson Jones, Ryan Searles and Robert Ruggeri.

And to Ivan Schwarz, who, back in late 2008 offered to look at the script, read the rawest first draft, saw something in it and sent me on my way to LA.

Sometimes one Yes is all it takes.

HAIR: ROSA WILSON

ABOUT THE AUTHOR: ALEX SUKHOY

Woman.

Mother.

Sister.

Daughter.

Granddaughter.

Cousin.

Niece.

Friend.

Neighbor.

Writer.

Marketer.

Educator.

Coach.

Mentor.

Artist.

Musician.

Traveler.

Immigrant.

Citizen.

Survivor.

Journal Addict.

Glorification of Women's Domestic Obligations as the Opportunity Cost of Pursuing One's Dreams?

Fuck ALL that shit.

Forever.

ABOUT THE CONTRIBUTOR: JACOB LIVSHULTZ

Man.

Husband.

Father.

Brother.

Son.

Grandson.

Cousin.

Nephew.

Friend.

Writer.

Educator.

Artist.

Traveler.

Hockey Dad.

Immigrant.

Citizen.

Social Niceties?

Fuck that shit.

Generational Trauma.
She’s a real cunt.

Order your copies of Episodes 1 and 2 from Amazon:

★★★★★ **Can't wait to read Episode 2!**
Reviewed in the United States on February 16, 2022
Verified Purchase

Engaging saga of a family over generations that dovetails against a post industrial rust belt city. This is a real page turner. Clevelanders will have fun recognizing inside references. Looking forward to the next Episode.

★★★★★ **Captivating screenplay**
Reviewed in the United States on July 8, 2022
Verified Purchase

The story is captivating and the characters are well developed. Once I started reading, I couldn't put the this screenplay down. I can't wait to see what happens in episode 2!

★★★★★ **Ambitious storytelling**
Reviewed in the United States on May 28, 2022
Verified Purchase

This first episode lays out the characters and context for intertwining and sordid stories. It's fun to imagine how this story (and Cleveland) will translate to the screen. Really appreciate the attention to detail with Cleveland's history and the soundtrack. Would love to read episode 2!

★★★★★ **A truly unique experience**
Reviewed in the United States on July 14, 2023
Verified Purchase

Episode 2 of the Girl From Cleveland City continues the story and delves deeper in to the past of our heroine while moving the story forward in a much needed and intriguing return to noir. The multi-faceted storytelling mixes a variety of methods to carry us along this mysterious journey.

★★★★★ **Wow! Can't wait for Episode 3.**
Reviewed in the United States on February 17, 2023

This is an epic story. Multiple time periods, rich in detail, a genuine mystery add up to a real page turner. After I finished Episode 2, I went back and reread Episode 1. Now, I am anxious for Episode 3. I need to know how the puzzle fits together. This would make a great film.

★★★★★ **The River Caught Fire!**
Reviewed in the United Kingdom on March 19, 2022
Verified Purchase

A generation spanning tale of Cleveland and the dynastic family around which the plot spirals. As with any script this will mutate and evolve over time, but the foundations are solid; setting up the intrigue, the secrets and red herrings for future episodes to reveal, resolve or possibly bury.

The script part of the book establishes the dramatis personae but centres on the enigmatic Esti.

My favourite element of the whole package, however, is the author's commentary - part memoir, part photo album, part provocation, but setting out the astonishing context in which such a tale could unfurl. I've never been to Cleveland, or the USA for that matter, but apparently the Cuyahoga river ACTUALLY CAUGHT FIRE!! And not only once. Such a sleasy civic backdrop of land deals and political maneuverings practically ensures that future episodes will expose Esti's and her family to a dark and potentially lethal denouement.

Other ★★★★★ Titles by Alexsandra Sukhoy:

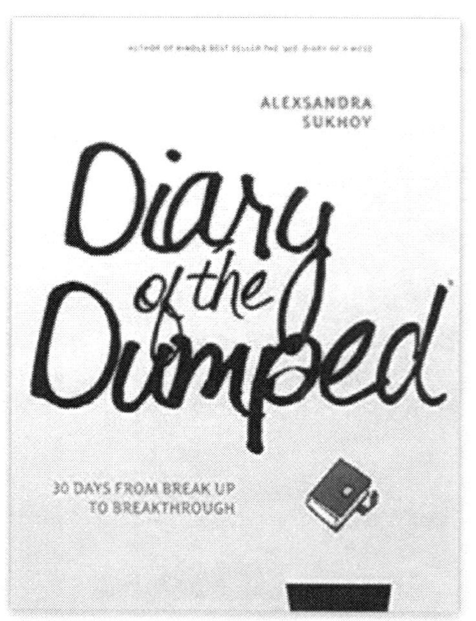

amazon.com/stores/Alexsandra-Sukhoy/author/B006TM4TCS

Made in the USA
Columbia, SC
03 June 2024